Beanstalk Books

Series Editor: Alan Blackwood
© 1975 Thomas Nelson & Sons Limited
SBN: 72381121 0
Printed in Great Britain by W. S. Cowell, Ipswich

WHERE'S CHARLIE?

Written by

Alan Blackwood

Illustrated by

Joan Beales

NELSON YOUNG WORLD

My Uncle Jim gave me a special prese
for my birthday. He said it was a
animal. It was in a small box. I thoug
it might be a snake or perhaps a hai
bird-eating spider. But Uncle Jim sai
"Go on, take the lid off. He won't bi
you."

I looked inside the box. There was the funniest looking animal I had ever seen.

"He's called a 'kam-me-lee-on'," said Uncle Jim. "That's how we say his name, but it's spelt 'chameleon'."

He lifted him out of the box and put him on my hand. The chameleon had a long tail, which he twisted round my finger. I knew at once that we were going to be friends.

"I think I'll call him Charlie," I said.

Mum was interested in Charlie, too. She said he was a funny little monster.

"Look at his eyes," Uncle Jim said. "They're quite different from ours. They don't only look different. They work differently too. See, each eye is looking in a different place."

"What food does Charlie like?" I asked.

"Flies," Uncle Jim said. "He has a long sticky tongue which he keeps curled up inside his mouth. Then, when he's hungry, and he sees a fly, he shoots out his tongue as fast as lightning and catches it."

"I'm glad he does something useful," Mum said.

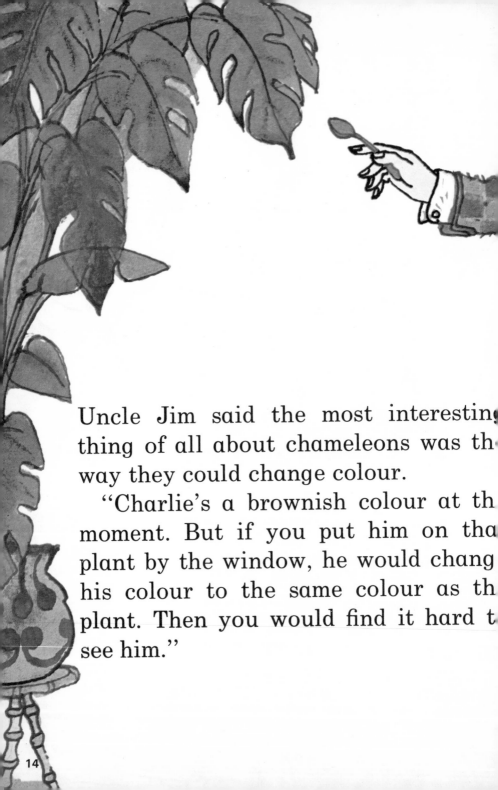

Uncle Jim said the most interesting
thing of all about chameleons was the
way they could change colour.

"Charlie's a brownish colour at the
moment. But if you put him on that
plant by the window, he would change
his colour to the same colour as the
plant. Then you would find it hard to
see him."

Great Uncle
Julian in Paris

So I put Charlie on the plant. He seemed quite happy there.

Then Uncle Jim looked at his watch and said he'd have to go. I was sorry to hear that, because I like Uncle Jim.

"Yes," Mum told me, "and you'd better get washed. Your Aunty Edna's coming to tea."

I was sorry to hear that, because I don't like Aunty Edna. She talks about other people all the time. She never actually says anything nasty about them, but I think she'd like to. And she's got a horrid little dog called Ming. He's always sneezing and yapping. He gets cross, and sometimes he bites.

When Aunty Edna arrived, she bent down to kiss me. It was a very wet kiss.

"Happy birthday, luvvy," she said, and gave me a pair of socks.

"Go and talk to your aunty while I get the tea things ready," Mum told me.

I hate having to talk to Aunty Edna. She talks to me the way she talks to Ming. She must still think I'm some sort of a baby. But I'll bet there are lots of things I know that she doesn't.

I helped Mum bring in the tea things. Ming started yapping.

"Be quiet Ming," Aunty Edna said. She picked up the largest cream cake on the table, and started giving bits to Ming. There were crumbs all over the chair, and blobs of cream on the floor.

Then Aunty Edna drank a cup of tea. When she thought nobody was looking, she turned round to drop the tea leaves from her cup into the plant pot. But I was looking, and so was Charlie.

Charlie moved a little bit. Aunty Edna let out a kind of shriek.

"What is it, what is it?" she screamed, pointing at Charlie.

Ming started yapping again, jumped off the chair and got his lead caught up with the cake stand. The big jam cake which Mum had made for my birthday fell right into Aunty Edna's lap.

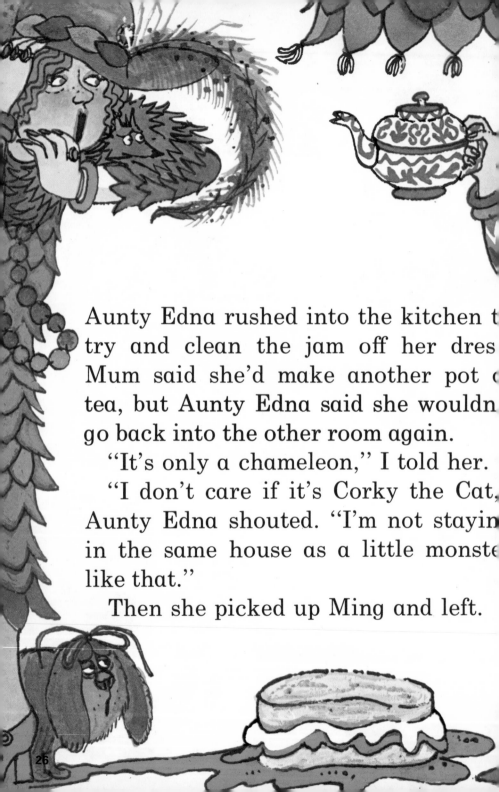

Aunty Edna rushed into the kitchen t
try and clean the jam off her dres
Mum said she'd make another pot o
tea, but Aunty Edna said she wouldn
go back into the other room again.

"It's only a chameleon," I told her.

"I don't care if it's Corky the Cat,
Aunty Edna shouted. "I'm not stayin
in the same house as a little monste
like that."

Then she picked up Ming and left.

We haven't seen Aunty Edna since. I think Mum's almost as pleased as me that she hasn't come back. She doesn't say so, of course.

It's all thanks to Charlie, really. He's like one of the family now. And yesterday he caught his first fly. I was glad about that. I was getting worried, in case Aunty Edna had put him off his food.